Puckered

Other David Owain Hughes Titles

Novels, Novellas and Short Story Collections:
All-Wound Up
Wind-Up Toy
Wind-Up Toy: Broken Plaything
Wind-Up Toy: Chaos Rising
White Walls and Straitjackets
Escapees and Fevered Minds
Choice Cuts
Walled In
Man-Eating Fucks
The Rack & Cue
Collision Course
Granville
Home Improvements

Anthologies:
Shadows and Teeth Vol.3
Trapped Within
Hell of a Guy
Unleashing the Voices
Rejected for Content Vol. 4, 5 & 6
Crossroads in the Dark Vol.1 & 2
Fifty Shades of Slay
How to Cook a Baby
Madame Movora's Tales of Terror
Big Book of Bootleg Horror Vol. 1, 2 & 3
Shopping List
Depraved Desires
Easter Eggs and Bunny Boilers
Bah! Humbug!
Slashing Through the Snow
VS Vol. 1 & 2
Black Candy
Into the Abyss

Compiled & Edited Anthologies:
What Goes Around
Man Behind the Mask
Fuck the Rules

Puckered

By

David Owain Hughes
&
Peter Oliver Wonder

Edited by
Jonathan Edward Ondrashek

A HellBound Books Publishing LLC Book
Houston TX

A HellBound Books LLC
Publication

www.hellboundbookspublishing.com

Printed in the United States of America

Dedication

I'd like to dedicate the novella to my children, Gethin David Hughes and Ruby Storm Leigh Hughes.

Puckered

Puckered

Puckered

THE SPOON SCRAPED at the bottom and sides of the bowl, trying to get every last morsel of the refried beans. His belly was stretched as far out as he could ever remember. A satisfied grin spread across his face. The release wouldn't be too far off now.

He squirmed as his anus threatened to let loose what he had worked so long to perfect. The squeak of a slow, methodical fart let its way out and he thanked the gods that a fart was all it was. Once the stench of his flatulence reached his nose, he jiggled and shook as he laughed.

"Goddamn it, Percival! That is vile! How many times have I told you to not do that at the dinner table?" the woman chastised her 36-year-old son as she reeled away. "I invited you back into my home after you got evicted from your last place, expecting a certain degree of respect from you. This is unacceptable! You don't pay rent, you won't help with chores, and worst of all, your filthy sense of humor is deeply disturbing. I don't know why you do the things you do, but I don't have to sit here and take it! Since you do absolutely nothing all day, could you at least clear the table?"

Still laughing, he mumbled, "Are there any more beans left?" Wet, brown chunks of the meal spewed forth as he spoke to the backside of his mother before she exited the room.

A pain somewhere inside his intestines caused the laughter to stop as beads of sweat joined together on his greasy forehead and slithered down his nose. He leaned forward to move the pressure of the massive shit that had been building up for the past three weeks. His previous record had been a week and a half, but that was before he'd read a story about a sixteen-year-old girl who'd had a fear of toilets, held her stool in for eight weeks, and ended up having a heart attack due to an enlarged bowel.

"Oh, no, Percy. This one isn't ready yet. There's work yet to be done before the main star is ready to take stage." Now that the cramp had subsided, he carefully stood and made his way around the table and over to his mother's spot, where scraps still remained on her plate.

Tacos were, by far, his favorite meal with which to sculpt his loaves. The grease helped coat his stomach, the meat and beans helped to grow the beasts, and the fiber in the lettuce helped keep it all bound together. Holding shit in until it gets to an uncomfortable amount is one thing, but crafting the perfect turd is another feat in itself. With one misstep, a huge dump could turn into hot espresso spewing forth from one's ass. A step in the other direction could result in a solid brick that would rip a man's asshole straight down to his ballsack.

Percy learned both of these things the hard way over the course of several years. When you get a taste for dropping massive bombs, there aren't many sources for information—you don't simply find someone with similar interests at the grocery store who winds up being your mentor. When you eat to craft massive bowel movements, everything you do is self-taught through trial and error, and sometimes those errors can cost a man much more than money. Percy had put blood, sweat, and tears into honing his craft, and his latest offering would be his most prized creation to date.

Now that he was in his thirties, Percy assumed he had seen every type of defecation that could be produced by the human body, from explosive diarrhea to bricks that refused to budge, to feces that were more akin to a light, spongy soufflé than human excrement. Experimentation was key in crafting the perfect poo.

Of course, the aesthetic beauty of his creations was not the most important part. No, what Percy was after was the sensation of pushing that thick log from his anus for as long as possible. The squirts were messy and, even worse, caused his cornhole to burn as if it had been stuffed with ghost peppers before receiving a long spray of mace by a rape victim. The solid shits were what he truly desired. He didn't want it to form so solidly that he had to take a stool softener to force it out, but a little more solid than an average crap. He liked the feel of lesions forming as his anus stretched beyond its maximum diameter.

As he slurped the last of the refried beans from his finger, his phone vibrated in his pocket, giving his testicles a lovely, tingly sensation and enticing his pecker to perk up. He reached inside and held the phone firmly to his genitals for a few buzzes before pulling it out. "This is Percy."

"Percival F. James?" the voice on the other line clarified.

"Yes. What's all this about?" He rolled his eyes, annoyed. The man's professional voice had forced his semi to fade back to a flaccid wad of flesh between his legs.

"This is Detective Brown. There has been an incident at 221 Baker Street, which happens to be your former residence. Is that correct?"

"Yeah, I used to rent a room there."

"As I said, there has been an incident and I was given your name. I was hoping you could come down to the station to answer some questions. No one is accusing you of anything. We just need some assistance filling in the blanks, is all."

Percy sat quiet and thoughtful for a moment. He had no interest in helping the police in any way whatsoever. On the other hand, he also had no interest in helping his mother by clearing the table. For him, it was amusing to watch her struggle and try to push him into doing chores or errands. He felt as if she might actually kick him out sometime if he didn't start doing stuff for her every now and then. This, however, was a golden opportunity to continue doing nothing.

"Yeah, I'll be there shortly."

"Thank you, Mister Ja—"

Percy shut off the phone and placed it back into the pocket of his stained sweatpants.

"Ma, I can't clear the table, sorry. I have to go to jail. The police just called me." A slimy grin covered his face as he pushed away from the table. He loved the disappointed reactions his mother had to offer.

"Oh, goddamn it, Percy," she groaned as she stormed nearer. "I always knew this was coming. What the hell did you do? Did you kill someone's kitten or beat up some little kid at the park?"

Both knees audibly popped over the sound of his laughter as he stood. "Ma, why would you say these things to such an upstanding citizen? They called me asking for my assistance in an ongoing investigation. I haven't done anything wrong and I don't appreciate your accusations." His face carried the same slimy smile as he walked past her and toward his bedroom.

"Bullshit," she said, despising the joy that was pasted to his face. She knew full well that he had tortured and killed small animals and bullied and even hit young children for no other reason than the fact that he enjoyed such things. "Just tell me what you've done so I don't have to hear it from the police. You know that will break your mother's heart, Percy," she said, following him to his room.

Percy slammed the door before she could enter. On the small table was a bottle of lotion, a sock (which had not a single spot that was not encrusted in old semen), his wallet, and a folding knife. He tossed the last two items into his pockets.

"Nope, not this time, Ma," he said, opening the bedroom door once more. "I'm one of the good guys this time. Look at me, heading off to help the police! Aren't you proud of your boy? Oh, that reminds me," he said, forcing the smile from his lips. "It sounded pretty important. Actually, it sounded *really* important. Someone might even be dead. Think you could take care of the table and the dishes for me?" He pushed past her in the narrow hall and the despicable smile crept back to his mouth.

"No, no, *no,* Percy! You are not a child anymore and I'm not going to let you act like one! The dishes are going to be right here for you when you come back!" she shouted as the front door slammed shut.

Downstairs, Percy felt like the king of the world—the bus was pulling up just as he was leaving the building. No dishes, no waiting around, and no accidental sharts even though three weeks of held-in shit was just around the corner. As he waddled, the bus lowered before the door opened inward, folding accordion style.

The bus was overcrowded, which was a blessing and a curse for Percy. He abhorred people, but oh, how he loved to make them squirm.

He walked down the aisle, making no effort to avoid bumping into other riders. The driver released the brake, which jarred Percy as he continued shuffling toward the center of the bus. The sudden motion caused the contents of his colon to shift uncomfortably. He ceased his rearward movement and grasped onto the overhead rail as he tried to settle his stomach. He was certain something had shaken loose and prayed to the porcelain gods that it was only a fart and that his bowels wouldn't relieve themselves right there.

With caution and determination, he tried to alleviate the pressure in his gut. Though he typically had tremendous control over what came out of his asshole, unclenching his puckered stink-ring was always a dangerous gamble—especially in a confined place such as public transportation. With monk-like focus, he tried to squeeze the volatile gas from his body. When the heat began to silently fill his sweatpants without any weight or moisture, he felt quite pleased with himself, but not as pleased as he would be after what was about to come.

In the confined space, the other passengers shifted and their faces contorted into expressions of pain and revulsion. One young woman, likely in her early twenties, gagged and dry-heaved before making her way further toward the rear of the bus. It was almost impossible for Percy to contain his joy. Maintaining the stoic poker face was a feat in itself. The stench that filled the small area was like a mustard gas canister going off in a trench. The sight of watering eyes caused a stifled chortle to escape him.

Another squeak, like the sound of rusted hinges being opened, forced its way out of Percy's backside as the bus hit a pothole. He puckered his anus tighter than a nun's cunt, fearing his load was going to drop there and then. Sweat beaded across his forehead and trickled down either side of his face, finding its way into his ears and up his nostrils, which flared like a horse's as he breathed in and out heavily.

Calm down, he thought. *It will pass.*

A deafening grumble in his gut erupted, like a pot boiling over on a stove—someone from behind muttered something about the smell and sounds coming from Percy, but he didn't catch it all. He was too busy trying to keep his shit in.

Fuck, fuck, fuck! I don't think I can stop it!

He gripped the rail on the seat in front of him so tightly that his fingers turned white.

Breathe!

He started panting like a pregnant woman in labor, not caring how it must have looked to the people around him.

Another pothole.

A second explosion in his guts.

Oh, Jesus!

More pops, bangs, and squeaks escaped him—it sounded like a gunfight, like someone or some heinous thing was letting off hand grenades inside him. And then, just like that, it passed. His guts settled like the calming of an ocean, without a ripple in sight.

His grip on the bar relaxed. Color returned to his fingers as his blood started to circulate once again.

Percy licked away his sweat moustache and let out a heavy sigh. He squirmed in his shirt, which was plastered to his moist back, and then plucked at the saturated thighs of his sweatpants. As he fidgeted in his seat, he felt the sogginess in his underwear, which he put down to perspiration and not that he'd shit himself.

Although, I have been fooled before!

Slowly, Percy lifted himself off the seat so his ass was hovering a few inches from the padding. He put a hand behind him and to his rear and then pushed at it. Satisfied there was no shepherd's pie in his pants, and indeed the turtle had stopped poking its head out of its shell, he lowered himself back down gently.

His mouth made the perfect O shape as he did so.

I think I'm starting to get a bit of ring-sting!

He smiled at how positively disgusting he was.

I wonder if the young lady at the back would like to smell and lick my shitty fingers clean!

A schoolgirl-like titter burst from him, forcing him to stifle it by clamping his hand over his mouth and nose, turning it into a piggy snort. Once he had himself under control, Percy relaxed in his seat and tried to restrain his excitement regarding how long he'd managed to contain his waste.

Percy's aim to shatter the current eight-week record was well on course, and when it did finally explode free, he knew his orgasm would be monumental. He also knew there would be no need to stroke his cock because the jizz would shoot out of him along with his excrement.

He'd been practicing.

Conditioning his body.

It had taken Percy the best part of ten years to get to this stage; to reach a level of control over his body that was nothing short of Zen-like.

I am the Master of Movements! he thought, smiling.

And then his mind reeled. Just when did this obsession, or rather perversion, start?

His forehead furrowed.

Last year of school? His face flushed at the memory, heating his cheeks and neck. *I've come a long way since then . . .*

***

"You going to fuck her in the ass, man?"

"Fucking right, Jason."

"Yeah, yeah, Robert—you know how much of a fucking prude Kelly is. But you ain't even stuck your fingers in her pussy or your tongue down her throat yet!"

"How about you suck on this, dickface!"

Percy dared to look over his shoulder at the other lads—he saw Robert giving Jason the middle finger—before turning his head back to face front. *Keep your eyes on the tiles and they'll leave you alone,* he thought.

"Wow! Your dick is starting to grow just thinking about Kelly, Rob. Hey, Matt, take a look – Rob's getting a stiffy."

"Fucking perv," Robert said, laughing.

Percy then heard a noise that sounded like flesh on flesh.

"Ow, man! No need to deaden my fucking arm."

"That'll teach you to look at another man's joint of beef."

The boys all laughed.

Block them out, Percy thought, soaping his body. *Just . . .* The sensation of needing to push a shit out washed over him, causing his knees to buckle slightly. He collapsed against the wall and panted like a dog at its bowl. *No! Not here. Not now.*

His thighs quaked as he clamped his ass cheeks together, forcing the crap back up inside him. Sweat poured out of him.

Sweet fuck! It feels so good.

Percy closed his eyes and let the pleasure take over, feeling his stool rub against his g-spot. He lightly pushed again, his waste trying to flee. Before it could, he sucked it back up inside. Another wave of gratification washed over him.

He bit his lip.

The sound all around him faded away.

When he opened his eyes, he noticed his vision had become blurry and tunnel-like.

The soap he was holding skyrocketed out of his hand when he squeezed it, causing it to ricochet off a shower head and then bounce off a water-drenched wall before coming to a stop in a puddle of water at his feet.

Control it now! Keep it in!

Percy had been cooking this stool since he'd left the house that morning, and it was currently a record for him: almost six hours.

Even though he hadn't come, these short bursts of forcing and then retrieving his crap from the brink of shooting into his pants were orgasmic in a different way; it was exhilarating. However, throughout the day, pre-come had moistened the tip of his penis, causing his underwear to glue themselves to him.

At that moment, a fart squeaked out of him, which sounded deafening in the confined shower room.

"Oh, fuck!" Percy uttered, his whole body shaking as another contraction washed over him. His guts cramped and then flip-flopped. "I need the toilet! It's *coming!*" His toes dug into the tiled floor. He placed his head and arms against the wall in front of him and scrunched his eyes closed. "Ooh!" he cried with delight, his turd galloping down his shit-chute.

"What the fuck is James doing?!" Robert yelled, and then laughed.

"He's shaking like a shitting dog!" Jason commented.

"*Sir!* I think James is pulling his dick!" Matt bellowed.

All the boys laughed, jeered, and threw insults at Percy, who could do nothing but try and control his bowel movement.

"I don't think I can stop it!" he gasped.

"What did he say?!"

"Something about fucking his mother!"

The boys erupted into another bout of frenzied laughter.

"What the fuck is all the noise in here?!" Mr. Lewis demanded. "This is gym class, not fuck-off class!"

"Sir, it's James! He's playing with himself!"

"Help!" Percy said, looking over his shoulder and finding his gym teacher. "I'm in agony! Ugh!" His guts spasmed and his eyes rolled. Something trickled down his legs, which wasn't water from the shower head, as he wasn't standing under it any longer.

Percy looked down. Shit-colored liquid, which was mixed with blood and miniscule chunks of food, slid down his calves.

"Urgh!" one of the boys exclaimed.

"Fucking sweet corn!" another yelled.

"No fucking shitting in my showers, James!" Mr. Lewis said.

"I-I can't help it," he said, feeling another convulsion rock his body.

"I think I'm going to chuck my guts!" Matt said.

Percy slipped down the wall, his nails raking the porcelain. A lump of shit found its way out of his ass, which had become loose—he was now unable to pucker.

The excrement splashed into a pool of water.

"Holy fuck!" Robert said, tossing his soap at Percy. "You dirty little cunt."

"Get him the hell out of there!" Mr. Lewis yelled.

Percy felt rough hands all over him, and then he was being dragged across the shower floor. As he went, he left behind him a brown, slug-like trail. He was powerless trying to stop the attack, as another bout of orgasmic joy racked him. "Feels so good!" he whispered.

His eyes flicked open, and it briefly registered that he was being hauled through the locker room.

"W-w-where are you . . ." he said, unable to finish his sentence.

"He's shitting all over the fucking floor!" someone claimed.

"Always knew he was a rancid fucker," another lad said.

"That's enough," Mr. Lewis said.

"His dick's hard!" a third person joined in.

"What should we do with him, Robert?"

"Let's throw him in the girls' changing room."

Mr. Lewis laughed. "I never saw this, remember."

"We won't snitch, sir. Besides, this cunt's had it coming for years," Robert stated.

"N-n-no . . . Please," Percy said, but he couldn't do anything to stop it, as more shit came out of him.

He knew he was now outside the boys' locker room because it felt cold, the typical circulating warm mist from inside no longer existent. His dick shriveled as the horniness left him, and the urge to fight back came upon him like a tidal wave.

Within minutes, he was hoisted off the floor and dragged kicking and screaming towards the girls' changing room.

He screamed for Mr. Lewis' help, but it went unnoticed.

Bastard!

As his head flicked this way and that, he caught a fleeting glimpse of his shit-covered body—it looked as though he had been rolling around in mud like a piggy.

When the door to the girls' room came into view, he cried and begged for mercy, but it was of no use: Robert and the rest shoved him through it headlong. Percy screamed when his body scraped along the floor, skinning his knees and elbows.

The second round of humiliation began as Percy got to his hands and knees and looked up at the mass of half-naked and bare-assed girls who flanked him. Some were as bold as brass and stood with their hands on their hips, exposing everything to him.

"It's Pervy Percy!" Rachel Claireson said, pointing at him. "You stink like a bag of shit!" she continued, pegging her nose with her index finger and thumb.

"Noodle dick!" another girl said.

Percy quickly got to his feet and covered his privates.

The ladies burst into giggles and shrieks as he ran towards the door and tried to open it, but it wouldn't budge. "Let me out! *Please!*" he squealed, his voice cracking. Tears rolled down his cheeks.

"Fuck you!" Robert yelled, giggling on the other side of the door.

As Percy yanked on the handle, wrapped tampons and wet towels bounced off his back, head, ass, and shoulders.

"He has shit stuck in the hairs of his crack!" Rachel screeched.

"Ew! He's vile," another girl said.

"What's going on, girls?"

Percy recognized the new voice as that belonging to Ms. Goff. "Help!" he said, turning around and covering his cock and balls once again. He couldn't help but scan the naked tits and pussies about him, not that it interested him that much.

"My God, James! Get out of here, you little pervert."

"But Miss, it's not my fault! Robert Daniels and Jason Clarkson threw me in here. They won't open the door."

The rotund gym teacher pushed her way through the girls and towered over his scrawny body.

"Out of the way, *boy!*" she said, shoving him by his shoulder. When she grabbed the handle and pulled, the door flew open with ease. She whirled on him. "Locked, you say?"

"B-but . . . I swear—"

"Bloody pervert!" She grabbed him by the ear, twisted it, and marched out into the corridor and up to the boys' changing room. She rapped on the door with her stubby fist three times before Mr. Lewis opened it. "I found *this* in my girls' room, Mr. Lewis. This happened under your care?"

"I don't know what you're talking about. I didn't see anything—I was in the storeroom."

Percy's mouth hung loose.

The lying bastard!

"Get in there, clean yourself up, and get dressed. I'll be waiting here for you."

"W-why, Miss?"

"*Move!*" she bellowed.

He sauntered through the changing room, all the while covering his privates, and headed for the shower, where he rid himself of the smell and shit stains that covered his body—some had even gelled his hair.

When he was done and dressed, he met Ms. Goff outside and she marched him down to the headmaster's office. Afterward, he was sent home with a letter and a two-week suspension.

His mother had hit the roof and tanned his ass.

The incident in the shower didn't deter him. Even if it had, he wouldn't have been able to stop—the sensation felt too great. Besides, he couldn't let the one bad experience derail him. After all, it had been his first attempt at trying to withhold going to the toilet for a full day. *I wonder what it would be like to hold it in for hours and hours. Days, even?*

The very next day, being as he was off school for the next two weeks, Percy got back on the bike and started again.

After filling his gut with a big breakfast, snacks, and dinner, he sat around and waited for his loaf to cook. With his mother at work, he had the run of the place. And even though she'd left him a list of things to do while she was gone, he instead pissed around on his laptop, watched TV, and listened to music.

At six o'clock that evening, his shit oven pinged, informing him a bowel movement was imminent. Of course, he ignored it. Seven, eight, nine, and ten o'clock came and went, and still he hadn't used the toilet. By then his mother had returned from work and roasted him for ignoring his chores. She ordered him to bed, where he lay awake for as many hours as he could.

By three o'clock that morning he was rolling around in bed in agony. Even if he had wanted to get up to go to the toilet, he wouldn't have been able to: the cramps in his stomach were beyond any form of pain he had ever experienced, even worse than when he'd broken his knee in four separate places the previous summer.

"Oh, Jesus!" he said, grabbing his stomach.

Sweat poured down his face and dripped off his back and neck, soaking his sheets through to the mattress. The color drained from his face.

When five o'clock rolled around, Percy thought he was dying. The extreme heat that coursed through his body brought on a mild bout of delirium, which caused his mind to work overtime:

What if something has exploded inside me?

Maybe my system has become poisoned?

My organs are melting.

I'm going to be shitting blood and chunks of stomach for the rest of my life.

I'll never walk again.

23

My dick will fall off because of ass rot.

"Mum!" he called, but his voice was hoarse. "W-water . . ." Gasping, he sat up. A stabbing pain shot from his stomach to his chest, causing him to collapse back against his mattress. "Breathe," he told himself. "Relax. Panicking isn't going to help—it's just making things worse!"

Percy, with all his might and effort, pushed himself up and off the bed. Once he was on his knees, he managed to bend over to his window and open it. Cold air rushed into the room.

Relief washed over him.

He gently lowered himself back to his mattress, peeled his pajama top off, and lay as straight as a poker. With the air stroking his body, he was able to chill out—he allowed his mind to empty.

"Block out the pain and enjoy the feeling. I'm in charge. I'm the Master of Movements! No more accidents like the other day in school."

After lying in a meditative state for another hour, he managed to control the pain in his system. This enabled him to go back to enjoying the feeling of pushing and puckering. Within minutes, his dick hardened to a throbbing, aching stage.

Of course, this wasn't through ass contractions alone.

Percy had thought about the embarrassment he'd felt in school, and used it to his advantage. He also thought about all the naked tits, ass and pussies he'd seen, not to mention the look of disgust on Ms. Goff's face.

But, try as he might, he couldn't get himself to come without the aid of his hand. So, he'd pulled his pajama bottoms off and let his hardness spring free.

Before he'd started experimenting with his anus as a form of sexual pleasure, Percy had been a heavy masturbator, and had always kept a tub of hand cream by the side of his bed. Opening that pot now, he scooped some of the gooey stuff out and lathered his cock and hand with it.

He loved the smooth feeling it created against his bell-end as he slowly stroked. After turning onto his side, he inserted a finger on his other hand into his sore anus and prodded at his chocolate star gently.

"*Ooh!*" he gasped, provoking tears as he finger-fucked himself.

When the next contraction hit and he had to push, he felt his shit slide down his pipe and brush against his finger. As he puckered and vacuumed his turd back up, Percy used his digit to shove it back to where it had come from.

"*Ow!* Fucking hell! That feels so goddamn nice . . ."

His body contorted on the bed, making him look as though he were possessed.

He couldn't stop.

While still stroking his cock, Percy slipped his finger out of his ass and examined, sniffed, and even licked it. Some of his poop had found its way under the nail, and so he scraped it along the bottom row of his teeth and swallowed the muck.

"*Mmm!* Tastes like chocolate."

The smell heightened his sexual pleasure and desire to come.

He quickened his wanking pace, feeling his orgasm build.

"So . . . close . . ." he gasped as pre-come pooled around the tip of his cock. "Her . . . tits . . . were . . . so . . . big! Fucking slut!" Percy ground his teeth together and clenched them so hard that something clicked. "I'm coming! I'm coming!"

"Percy? Percy? What the hell is going on in there?"

In his moment of all-consuming, mind-numbing ecstasy, Percy didn't hear his mother knock on his door or call out from the other side.

"Answer me this second or I'm coming in!"

"N-no . . ." he uttered, unable to speak up due to the gasping and panting that racked his body. His bowels grumbled, and his stomach flip-flopped. A series of farts which sounded like staggered machine-gun fire left him. "I-I can't hold it back any longer! Oh, *Jesus!"* he yelled from behind clenched teeth.

His fingers and toenails dug into the mattress.

"What on earth are you doing, boy?! Stop that at once!"

When he rolled flat onto his back and opened his eyes, the shock at seeing his mother standing over him didn't register.

He was lost in his own little world.

And then it happened.

Percy arched his back and let go of his dick, which flopped about and shot semen in all directions like some kind of sprinkler system.

"Percy!" his mother screeched.

But he couldn't look at her because his anus was now releasing and spraying his bedding.

"Oh, *God!* I can't stop!" he screamed. "I think I'm bleeding!"

Then, he felt her rough hands on him. "Stop it, you dirty little bastard."

The flat of his mother's palm struck him across his right cheek, and then his left.

"You animal!"

"I-I couldn't help it . . ." he panted. "Is that you, Mum?" he pretended. "Feel my head—I'm burning up. When are we going to Disneyland?"

"Bloody hell, you're on fire!" she said, pressing the back of her hand to his forehead. "I'll call the doctor."

That evening, after the doctor had come, informed his mother that people did strange things in the grip of a fever, and left, she had told Percy that she didn't strictly believe what yarn he was trying to spin. And if she ever caught him in such a depraved way again, she would turf him out of the house.

"I blame that dirty beast of a father of yours. No-good drunken bum! All he left me with was a pittance and a pig for a son," she'd told him before leaving the room.

A smile had spread across his face.

Another loaf was building.

The day after, Percy marched onwards with his experiment. And, just like the accident in the shower and in front of his mother, they continued to happen as he honed his skill.

As the weeks flew by, he found himself able to hold his waste in longer. What started as a few hours turned into a day, then *days*, then a week. By the time his puckering skill was up to holding shit in for a fortnight at a time, Percy found he didn't need to touch himself to climax either: he made himself come by heightening the pleasure until he was so excited that it burst out of him.

A bit like a wet dream! he'd thought when he'd managed to pull it off for the first time.

***

Recalling the memory about shitting himself in front of his mother made Percy cackle. Another fart left him as the bus hit yet another pothole.

"*Ugh!*" a man protested from somewhere behind him. "What *is* that god-awful stench?!"

Percy continued to chortle, but stifled it somewhat. He was worried he might be heard and didn't fancy a pounding or argument.

God, that was a glorious night. I don't think I've ever had an ejaculate quite like that since. Well, they do say your first time is the best.

Back in the here and now, Percy noticed that the stop for the police station was only a few blocks away. He inhaled deeply and once more focused on his breathing. He needed to calm himself so as not to appear a sweaty, guilt-ridden mess before a questioning officer of the law.

One of the windows ahead of him was open, allowing a gentle breeze to blow through. The wind caught the tuft of thinning hair atop his head, causing it to sway this way and that. The glistening beads of sweat that adorned his forehead embraced the cool air and Percy enjoyed each individual drop as he entered his Zen-like state.

Above the roar of the busy city street, he heard birds chirping as they sat atop the power lines. Among the various scents in the air—car exhaust as well as the stench of his own gas—he was able to pick out the smell of the fresh-cut grass in the park on the other side of the street. It was a beautiful day outside and he felt it was his duty to appreciate the moment. If he didn't appreciate such beauty in the world, he felt it wouldn't be as satisfying when he enjoyed the truly disgusting things. Without the magic of nature, how would he enjoy the ugliness that could be displayed by humanity?

A sudden jolt was a gentle reminder that it was time to get off the bus. He stood from his seat, looking down to make certain his shit hadn't managed to escape. Upon the orange, molded plastic seat, clear moisture from the gross amounts of sweat covering him glistened. Percy smiled at the sight and shuffled toward the front of the bus, cautiously applying a crop-dust his whole way through the aisle.

The tall step was quite the obstacle to navigate with a gut so uncomfortably full. He grasped the rail and slowly stretched his leg down. The fresh air outside embraced him as his asshole once again shut itself, ending the stream of filthy heat that had been emanating from his backside.

His left foot dropped to the sidewalk, sending a ripple up his leg and throughout his frame. Making his way to the right, toward the police station, he saw there was a quaint little coffee shop just ahead. Outside it was an area for patrons to enjoy their offerings in the sun. Across the sidewalk from the gated area was a narrow tree with a red dog leash tied to it. On the other end of the leash was a small mixed-breed mutt that sat gnawing at his ass with tenacity.

Percy smiled at the dog. Not because he thought it was cute or funny, but because he knew he would always be stronger than such a creature. No matter what he could do to it, there was no real course of action the animal could take to gain its vengeance.

Focused intently on the mutt's exposed tail, Percy began measuring his steps as he pulled out his phone. He loved maintaining plausible deniability.

Watching the dog from over the top of his screen, he tapped away at the glass. It gave him a rush of adrenaline when he finally stepped on the dog's tail, twisting his foot as though it were nothing more than a cigarette butt as he did so. The animal's yelp caused the coffee shop patrons to turn their heads to find what appeared to be a sympathetic yet rushed Percy as he waved at the dog, saying, "Sorry there, pooch," before continuing on his path. Once out of view of the public, his greasy face contorted into a devilish grin as his genitals morphed from a flaccid flap to a half-chub inside his sweatpants.

After a few more paces, he placed the phone back into his pocket. The walking was causing his stinky brown passenger to bounce and threaten to dislodge itself. Realizing he was in no great rush, he slowed his pace. His destination was only one more block away and they weren't expecting him at a specific time.

Shuffling his way forward like a tortoise with a broken leg, Percy remained directly in the center of the sidewalk. This was a common practice for him; a man of his size was difficult to pass when off to one side as it was. A teenager on a skateboard, who had little to no chance of successfully navigating such an obstacle, entered his field of vision. The two met at the edge of the police station. The boy tried his best to get to the very edge of the sidewalk so he wouldn't have to slow down, but Percy was having none of it. He inched his way over until there was no way the boy could get by unscathed.

"Out of the way, you fat fuck!" Expecting the command to work, the kid stayed on his skateboard until he ran into Percy's shoulder and got flung into a bush. "What the fuck is your problem, asshole?"

"What's my problem?" Percy countered furiously. "What nerve you must have to question me. You've just come at me like a missile and then ask me what *my* problem is? Are you high on drugs?"

"Fuck you." The kid climbed out of the bush and readied his skateboard. "Have fun with your upcoming heart attack," he said before speeding off down the sidewalk.

Smiling from ear to ear, Percy grasped the railing and made his way up the stairs. Each step caused his cheeks to spread, and the brown prisoners being held within threatened freedom. He was glad the steps were short, unlike those of the bus. Still, he had to keep his butthole puckered to ensure his record-breaking shit would remain where it belonged.

He swung the door open and was greeted by a woman in a police uniform sitting behind a desk.

"Hiya, sweetheart. I'm here to see Detective Brown."

"First off, my name is Officer Jenkins, not sweetheart or anything else like that. Second, Detective Brown is down that way," she said, pointing to her right. "Third desk on the left."

"Thank ya, gorgeous."

The woman winced at the name, but decided to let it go as he set off in the direction she had indicated.

As he made his way towards the cluster of police and their various guests, Percy counted three times which desk was the third on the left only to conclude that it was, indeed, the black officer he was meant to speak to.

The officer looked up from his keyboard and noticed the large man standing in the aisle, staring at him. "Mr. James?"

Percy let out a grunt in reply.

"Won't you please have a seat?" Officer Brown asked with a friendly smile and a gesture to the seat.

To this, Percy gave no audible response. He simply began the snail crawl toward the indicated chair. Once there, he slowly lowered himself until his buttocks met its flattened seat cushion.

"Thank you for coming in so quickly, Mr. James," the officer began. "Now, you told me you did, in fact, live with one Mr. Kort. Is that correct?"

There was something, besides the color of his skin, that Percy didn't like. He wasn't sure if he was being overly friendly or what exactly it was, but Percy just wanted to get the interview over with. "Yeah, that's right. Up until about a week ago when he kicked me out. What's this all about?"

"All the way up until last week, you say?" Officer Brown asked, tapping away at the keys before him. "And are you aware of the cat that Mr. Kort calls his?"

As soon as the question left his mouth, the memory came back to him. Percy gulped, recalling the last time he'd seen it.

***

Three weeks ago, Percy had been having a difficult time holding his shit in after an excessively greasy meal. He was furious and when he made his way into his room, he found the cat lying asleep next to his bed, purring peacefully.

His lips had curled into an evil smirk as he slinked over to it, careful not to wake the thing. Looking down on it, he saw that all four legs were stretched out and touching at one point, making a triangle with the rest of its body. Percy lifted his right leg as high as he could manage and stomped down on all four of its legs with all his might. Bones shattered, completely obliterated, before the cat woke in shock. It twisted this way and that but was unable to move from its place on the faux-wood floor.

Satisfied that it wouldn't be escaping any time soon, Percy turned his back on the crippled animal and made his way to the kitchen. In the cutlery block, he found a pair of scissors which he took back with him to the room. Left completely defenseless, the cat tried to claw at Percy with its limp, lifeless legs, but quickly gave up. Instead, it tried to bite his hand as he gripped its tail.

He took the scissors to the end of the tail and snipped it off.

The cat got its jaws around a piece of Percy's hand and opened up a gash. "Ah, goddamn it!" he shrieked before backhanding the cat. It lay there in a daze, crying out as he snipped the end of the tail again and again. Once he was finished with the tail, he snipped off the ears, nose, and each of its feet before slicing it down its belly and pulling the skin completely off. He wasn't sure at which point the cat died—he'd been having too much fun torturing it to notice something so trivial.

Once he was finished with his fun, he took the cat, stuffed it in a plastic bag, and tossed it in the dumpster. Having disposed of the body, all that was left was to mop up the blood and bandage his injured hand.

***

"Yeah, I remember the cat. What about it?"

"Mr. Kort says he hasn't seen it in some time. When is the last time you remember seeing it?"

Percy sat silent for a moment, glaring hatefully at the policeman. "It's hard to say, but I believe the last time I saw it was the day I left. I'm pretty sure the little fluffball was weaving between my legs as I was grabbing the last of my things. Please don't tell me something has happened to him."

"That's interesting," said the detective as he sat back into his chair. "When I spoke to Mr. Kort, he mentioned you to me. He didn't have many nice things to say about you. In fact, he said you were one of the rottenest people he'd ever had the displeasure of meeting. He said you were cruel to the cat every time you were given the opportunity—kicking it away from you whenever it drew near. Are you saying these things aren't true?"

Percy squirmed in his chair, feeling his shit press against his anus. "Well, to be honest, I'm not sure if that's all fair. I didn't ever kick the cat. I'd try to pet it with my foot before it trotted off. It was a game between us. If that was misconstrued by my former landlord, that's not something I can take the blame for, now is it?"

"No, I don't suppose it is," the detective said. "However, there is the matter of the blood Mr. Kort found in your old room. Can you explain its presence there?"

Percy slowly shook his head. "No, I don't suppose I can. Have you any idea just how long that blood might have been there? To be frank with you, I didn't often lie on the ground in my room. Call me daft, but I far prefer the bed."

The detective nodded as an accusatory look spread across his face. After another glance at the screen before him, he stood from the desk, smiling once more. "I think that'll be all for now. Sorry to have you come all the way down here for something that seems to be so minor. Please, don't hesitate to contact us with any other information you may think of." He extended a hand to shake.

"Yeah, I'll be sure to do that," Percy said, slowly standing. He looked at the officer's hand before turning his back and heading out the way he had come. He was angry and had lost all joy from knocking over the boy on the skateboard. He needed something to cheer him up after having been accused of a crime he had, indeed, committed.

In front of the police station, he caught a whiff of something wonderful. Rather than feeding his rage, he figured he could feed his project-shit. The thought of pushing it out raised the corners of his mouth as well as the front of his trousers.

Across the street, he saw attached to the building a vertical red sign with yellow writing that read Tasty Palace in both English and Chinese characters. A quick peek at his watch confirmed what his stomach already knew: it was time to eat. Glancing each way, he decided to jaywalk across the street. The path was clear as he crossed the first lane. In the second, however, there was a woman in a minivan. Percy made eye contact with her as he slowed his pace before her vehicle. She smashed down on the horn, very nearly causing him to shit his pants right then and there. Startled, he slammed a fist onto her hood before scurrying the rest of the way to the other side of the street.

The moisture that saturated his underpants caused him another wave of panic. It was hot and he had already been sweating copious amounts, but this wetness felt as though it had a warmth of its own. He cautiously and hurriedly made his way into the Chinese restaurant and went right past the "Please wait to be seated" sign.

"You want table?" asked the man behind the register.

"Bathroom," Percy barked back.

"Bathroom for paying customer only!"

"Get me a table, then, but I'm going to the bathroom right now," he replied over his shoulder.

The employee was furious but knew he had no chance of stopping Percy, who showed no sign of obeying anything or letting anyone stand in his way.

Parallel to the kitchen was a hallway which led to the bathrooms. He swung the door inward before locking it behind him. He turned his backside to the toilet before yanking down his sweatpants and soaking-wet tighty whities and plopping down. The pressure on his anus was intense and he was half-tempted to cut the deuce right then and there before remembering why he came into the bathroom.

"Not yet, Percy. We're not done with this one just yet," he said. With his forearm, he wiped the sweat from his forehead before leaning forward to inspect the piece of cloth which was supposed to keep any shit from transferring from his asshole to his sweatpants. The once-white material was now stained and streaked with various shades of brown and yellow. He placed it between his thumb and fingers and gave it a squeeze. The sweat must have been heated from his own body warmth, which was a huge relief.

He gave the underpants another good squeeze, sending several drops of sweat falling to the uneven tile floor. Next, he raised his hand to his nose and took a deep breath. "Sweet Jesus, yes!" With his other hand, he reached between his legs, past his ballsack, and wiped the sweat from his taint. Beads of it dropped from his fingers and plopped into the water below. Cupping his hand tightly so as not to lose any more of the liquid, he brought the mess to his mouth and licked all the hot, salty, vile water away as though it was honey. Somewhere between his belly and his thighs, his johnson did a joyous dance as it stretched itself out.

Now certain he could continue holding in his payload, he dressed himself. He flipped on the faucet, and cupped his hands together to collect it and splash it into his face. The cool water was a huge relief. It washed away the annoyance of Detective Brown's questions and the scare he'd had in the middle of the street. He was no longer worried that he'd shit himself and he was ready to put something into his stomach. He splashed the water into his face one more time before shutting off the faucet and leaving the bathroom.

Exiting, he felt like a new man. Like an average man that wasn't filled with hatred, anger, and disgusting fetishes. A normal person, headed out to get some Chinese food for dinner. Though the tacos he'd had for lunch hadn't yet fully digested, he was more than happy to put something else delicious into his belly.

At a table in line of sight of the bathroom door stood the man who had insisted Percy dine in this establishment. The look on his face implied that he'd meant it when he said the bathroom was for paying customers only. Reinvigorated, Percy wasn't one to argue. "Table for one," he said coyly.

The man nodded and walked toward an open table in the middle of the restaurant. He set the menu that rested under his arm on the table and walked back to his station at the register before Percy even sat down. "Thank you," said Percy.

He opened the menu and balanced it on the table in front of him. Everything sounded so good, he thought he might be there for quite a while. Though it was warm out, he still wanted soup. Noodles and rice were a no brainer. For an entrée, it was a tough choice. He loved the Orange Beef, but the Sweet and Sour Pork was his favorite.

"Ready to order?" asked the man, who seemed to appear out of nowhere with a small notepad in his hand.

Percy collapsed the menu and said, "I'll have the number eight combo with a side of cream cheese wontons and an extra bowl of chow mein."

"Very good. I'll be back with your soup shortly."

Pleased with his meal choice, Percy sat back in his chair, which squealed under the strain of his weight. He placed his hands behind his head and gave his body a nice stretch while he gazed out the front door at the beautiful day.

A figure was silhouetted in the doorframe as they waited for help. "One, please," a man's voice said after gaining the attention of an employee. As the customer stepped away from the doorway, his face came into view. Percy pursed his lips, racking his brain. The man was familiar, but he didn't think it was anyone he had ever worked with and it sure as hell wasn't anyone he would consider a friend.

"Careful. Soup hot," said the waiter as he set the bowl down in front of Percy.

His previous train of thought derailed at the introduction of food. "Fantastic. Thank you," Percy said, dismissing the waiter before grabbing the spoon and ladling a wonton into his eager mouth. Though it was nearly hot enough to burn his taste buds, the flavors danced on his tongue like a playful nymph.

"Pervy Percy?!" exclaimed the same voice that had just asked for a table. It was directly behind him now.

The spoon stopped on its return trip to the table and remained in suspended animation as Percy tried to remember the last time he had heard the name he so despised. Though accurate, it had been the source of much grief in his adolescent years.

"Robert Nelson," Percy grumbled without turning to face the biggest bully he had ever known. His spoon was still frozen in space and time as he tried to prevent the growing anger within from getting the best of him.

"Holy shit, I *knew* it was you!"

Pompous laughter followed and felt to Percy as if it was filling all the space around him. The laughter of not just one man, but the laughter of an entire gymnasium all pointing at the boy covered in his own shit and come.

"How've you been, man?"

Percy turned to see a set of gleaming white teeth coming together to form a perfect smile.

"Oh, man. The years have not been kind to you, have they?" Robert said, laughing. "I'm sorry, that was rude of me. Seriously, though, how've you been?"

Percy caught sight of the blue uniform and badge which adorned Robert's chest. "You're a cop?"

"I am, and with perception powers like that, you ought to be a detective, buddy!" Robert continued laughing and enjoying himself as Percy's soup grew cold. "Oh, and speaking of detectives, I was talking to one of my cop buddies about this case about a guy who killed his old landlord's cat. Can you believe a person would do something like that?"

Percy didn't say a word. He just glared at his nemesis as his hands tightened into fists.

"I know, I know, I'm not supposed to discuss open cases with just anyone. Only thing is, you're not just anyone, are you, Pervy? You're the sole suspect in this animal abuse case, aren't you?"

"I don't know what you're talking about," Percy said, slowly lowering his spoon to the bowl.

"Oh, shit. I'm sorry, buddy. I didn't mean to interrupt your dinner. Please, continue enjoying your meal. Hey, what made you pick Chinese food, anyway? Is it because you think it's made from cat? *Meow!"* He burst into another fit of laughter before turning back to his own table.

A glance down at his spoonful of soup helped him realize he was no longer in the mood for Chinese food or anything else. With his appetite lost, Percy shoved his bowl of soup away, pushed his chair back, and then made a move to get up. A strong hand clamped his shoulder and forced him to sit back down.

"*Hey*! What the fuck, Rob? We aren't in school any longer—you can't bully or scare me with your intimidation tactics. I'll take you down," he dared to say, finding a steel in his gut he didn't know he possessed.

"Wow!" Rob smiled and removed his hand. "When did you find your balls?"

Percy made to get up once more but was again stopped by his former bully.

"You're pissing me off, Rob. Keep it up, and I'll have your badge on the grounds of police brutality. I'm pretty good at giving myself bruises."

The officer's mouth made a perfect O shape. "Are you threatening me, Pervy?"

Percy felt his hand inch across the table. His fingers curled around a steak knife.

I'll open up a fucking vein! he thought.

"No need for such hostility, Perc," Rob said, making the nickname rhyme with *purse*. He moved to the other side of the table, grabbed the chair there, and then dragged it over to Percy and sat by his side. "I thought that maybe we could be friends. You help me, and I'll help you," he continued, his hand moving across the table and resting on top of Percy's fat paw.

A tremble rocked through Percy's body.

His guts rumbled and his anus flexed.

A silent fart escaped him.

He's coming on *to me?! The jock is hot for cock! No . . . What the fuck is he up to?*

"Help you?"

"Tell me about the cat, Percy. I'm looking to crack this case. I want to impress Brown, see."

"You followed me here, didn't you?" He wanted to snatch his hand away, but didn't dare. He wanted to see how far Robert would push whatever sick game he was playing. *Come on, let's see what you got, big man!*

"Have you shit?!"

"Stop avoiding the fucking question!" Percy shot forward, pressing his nose to Robert's. "Answer me." The sudden movement caused his guts to twist and contract. Another fart broke cover and squeaked from beneath him. "Fucking chair needs oiling!"

Robert laughed. "You're disgusting. Do you realize how hard you made me in the shower that day? I went home and wanked like a fucking madman."

Percy drew back. The shock must have been plastered all over his face and jowls. "What are you saying, Rob? You're a fruit? The big bad ball player is a sausage jockey?! Oh my God!" Percy ripped his hand away and laughed in the guy's face, which turned scarlet. "And I—Ow!" he cried when Rob grabbed him by his ears and slammed his head against the table.

"Don't make me fucking hurt you more, Pervy Percy! You know what *they* like to do to tubby white boys behind bars? Hope your soap's on a rope."

"You motherfucker!" Percy wiped the blood from his nose. "I'll fucking kill you."

"Don't fight me, man. I want to be your friend." Robert stroked Percy's face. "I've always had a thing for you. If you did kill that cat, I can help you. But first, I need to know the full story. The truth."

He's trying to trick me . . . "What sick game are you playing here, Rob?" A powerful grumble assaulted his stomach, causing him to grip the sides of the table. "Oh, Jesus! I need to get to the toilet. It's coming," he panted. Sweat broke across his brow.

"Oh, God! You're still into the shit thing? You're making my prick hard all over again, man. You kinky fuck."

"I need to go. Out of my—"

"Not until you tell me what I want to know, Percy."

"No! You don't understand, Rob. Please!" A savage stabbing pain doubled him over. "Ow!" he cried, clutching his stomach.

"Let me help you then, Percy. Tell me what I need to know." Robert's hand returned to Percy's, who was distracted and in too much agony to care, even though, deep down, the affection was turning him on.

He felt a warm liquid trickle out of his ass. "I can't hold it back much longer," he whispered. "Please. I'm begging you."

"Give me the information and I'll let you go. I don't want to hurt you, Percy—I *want* you! I've always wanted you."

"What shit are you pull—Oh, fuck," he squealed, his guts bubbling and rumbling. "I feel as though everything is tearing open inside me!"

"You know what you've got to do to end this, man."

Percy's eyes fused with Robert's. "You promise you don't want . . . to . . . hurt me?" he gasped, breathing heavily. "You really *want* me?"

Robert smiled. "Of course. Didn't you ever see the way I used to look at you in the showers? I could never act on my feelings in school because all the boys looked up to me and the girls wanted to fuck me."

"You were with a different girl every week, man. You can't fool me by telling me you want dick!"

"That was a cover, silly."

"And your plan is to hold this cat business over me until I submit to you?"

"Come on, Percy. I know you secretly like boys. I can see it in your eyes. I bet your dick is bulging."

The cramps were becoming too much as more liquid trickled out of his ass and cut a path down the backs of his legs. His pants were saturated. "Ah!" he said, clutching the table tighter. His fingers dug so fiercely into the wood that his knuckles turned white.

A pressure built on his g-spot.

Pre-come gathered on the head of his cock.

"I'll tell!" he said, a loud fart acting as a full stop. "But I want your word that you will help me, Robert."

"You want to know how serious I am, Percy?"

Percy couldn't speak but managed a nod.

"Everything fine, sir?" the waiter asked.

"This is a police matter. Could you kindly cancel this gent's food order? I'll be taking him in for questioning soon."

"Very good, sir," the man said, moving away and taking the unfinished soup with him.

"I-I think . . . I'm having a heart attack!" Percy croaked, grabbing his chest. His breathing became erratic. Feverishly, he pulled at the collar of his shirt. "Water!"

"I'm not a fool, Percy. You're not having a heart attack. Now stop with the games! You're just making daddy's willy harder!" Rob winked, placing his hand back over the top of Percy's. "Now, tell—"

"I killed the cat. *There!*" His teeth were gritted together so tight that Percy thought they were going to shatter. "Now please, I need to use the toilet."

"Go right ahead." Rob smiled, reaching for the radio strapped to his chest.

When Percy tried to get up this time, he was forced back down due to the unbearable pain in his stomach.

"I'll help you in a second, Percy. Just need to call this in."

"Fucking little snitch! I knew I couldn't trust you."

"This is Officer Nelson. Could you patch me through to Brown, please? Over."

"Brown here. Over." The detective's voice sounded tinny coming through the walkie.

"I'm in pursuit of our cat killer, sir. Looks like we were wrong about Percy. Over."

"Where are you, Nelson? Who is it? Over."

Percy listened in shocked awe as Robert lied and manipulated his superior officer. *He wasn't lying about wanting me!* His elation didn't last long, as a wave of crippling pain washed over him, forcing him to topple off his seat and smash against the floor. "Help!" he howled.

The waiter came rushing over and knelt by Percy's side. "Sir! Sir! I call ambulance!"

Percy shook his head. "Get me to the toilet!" he pleaded.

"I'll handle it from here," Robert said, helping Percy to his shaking legs. "I have something that will help dislodge your problem, Percy."

"Why . . ." Percy panted, feeling himself being dragged across the restaurant floor, ". . . would you help me like that?" He felt the strength in his legs fade, and soon his toes were scraping along the floor as Robert continued to hold him up and steer him towards the bathroom.

"I told you, I like you. I've always liked you—bullying you broke my heart, Percy."

"You're so strong!"

They crashed through two swing doors and entered a room with brilliant white tiles, expensive-looking flagstones, and smart sinks with swanky fixtures.

"Jesus! Is he dying?!" someone asked.

"Get the fuck out of here, jackwagon," Robert yelled. "This is police business."

"Stall . . ." Percy said. He was then hauled into a small, tight space and placed against the toilet's septic tank.

"Take your trousers down, Percy—I'll be right back."

"Wha-what for?"

"I'm going to help you loosen that load, friend, and get us off at the same time. Now, drop 'em, cowboy."

He was in too much agony to argue, and so, with fragile movements, Percy untied the drawstring to his sweatpants. They fell down his legs and gathered at his ankles. He then heard a lock engage, followed by the stall door slamming shut and a second bolt locking into place.

"Got my nightstick all greased up with the hand soap, Perc."

"What?!" he almost screamed, glancing over his shoulder. The police baton looked like a giant black cock, and the way in which the pearl-white hand soap dripped off it reminded him of come. "Oh, Jesus! No, Robert!"

"It's either this or I haul you the fuck in, Percy. I believe you owe me for getting you off the hook . . ."

"But . . . but . . ."

"Relax. You'll enjoy it. Promise."

"What do you want me to do?"

Robert undid his belt and let his trousers hit the floor. "I want you to bend over so your ass is in the air."

Percy did what was asked of him, and placed his hands on the septic tank. Because his shit was pushing so viciously—causing pressure on his g-spot—he was horny. He needed a release, and this one had been a long time coming. To give Robert an extra thrill, he wiggled his wobbly, shit-encrusted ass at him. He wanted to speak, but he was concentrating too much on keeping his crap inside.

"Reach back and grab my cock, Percy."

He was almost surprised at how compliant he was. *Never thought I'd be up for trying anything like this!* he thought, reaching his hand back and finding Robert's stubby fat cock. *I always remember it being bigger! Then again, we were just boys back then.*

"That's it. Stroke it nice and gentle. Pet it."

Percy thought his legs were going to collapse from under him when a sharp jolting pain assaulted his rear-end. "Ah!" he gasped, and then settled. Once the nightstick was up his ass, he grinded and pushed back against it. "Oh, God!"

His dick stood to attention. Percy gently lowered his face onto the cold tank in front of him, so he could free up his other hand. He then started playing with his own cock as Robert fucked his ass.

A rumble in his stomach told him that something was soon to erupt.

"Harder, Rob—you're loosening everything!"

The faster Robert pumped, the quicker Percy's hands jerked their cocks.

"Shit, I'm almost there!" Robert squealed from behind clenched teeth.

Percy felt a hot stream of jism race up his back and plaster the backs of his legs.

The baton pulled free from his ass as Robert collapsed back against the stall door. As though the nightstick had been acting as a stopper, Percy's shit jettisoned out of his puckered ring and drenched his fuck-buddy, whose mouth was open as he gasped for air.

"Oh, fuck!" Percy cried, feeling everything rush out of his system. His cheeks flushed, and it seemed that every vein in his neck was protruding. Simultaneously, his prick erupted and redecorated the toilet seat.

The stench, even though he was spent, was almost enough to stir him hard again.

"Was that as good for you as it was for me, man?!" Robert said. "The fucking Earth moved."

Percy placed his shaking hands on the tank and then turned to look at Robert over his shoulder. His newfound friend was covered head to foot in liquefied shit that was riddled with peanuts and sweet corn. *Except he's not my friend*, he thought as ghosts from his troubled past breathed into his ear. *He never was and never will be.* "You would have been such a good playmate, but I can't trust you," he said, eye twitching.

"Huh?" Robert said, tipping his head to one side like a dumbstruck mutt.

"Goodbye, Nelson!" he yelled, ripping the ceramic lid off the tank and smashing Robert over the head with it.

Blood poured out of the man's cracked skull, reminding Percy of an egg with its crown broken off.

"This is going to be much more fun than offing a cat." He swung the hefty slab again and connected with Robert's jaw, which came clean off its hinges. Teeth pinged and rattled off the pan, walls, and floor, bringing a cartoon-like grin to Percy's wobbly chops.

The cop crumpled to the ground and held a pleading hand out in front of him.

"Oh, you're begging now? Just like I begged you to stop that day in the shower!" Percy screamed, bringing the porcelain down on the man's head again, and again, and again, until the slab snapped in half, sending chunks and shards in every direction.

After watching all of Robert's blood and color drain from him, Percy made his way out into the main section of the bathroom. He knew he couldn't just flee—too many people had seen him. And once Robert's body was discovered, it wouldn't be long before the authorities came to collect him.

Think, damn it!

Looking down at his ankles, he found his sweats. They were soaked in liquid shit and a police officer's blood. In front of him, the inside of the toilet was as clean as it had been when he had walked in—his spunk had landed on the seat, leaving the water within fresh and untouched. He kicked off the sweatpants, picked them up, plunged them into the toilet water, and did his best to clean them off.

The shit was an amalgamation of diarrhea and chunks of hard feces that had felt so good firing from his asshole like rounds from a BB gun. All the blood was layered on top of the brown mess and washed off at once. Next to fall away were the hard, brown chunks. A few tried to stick to the fuzzy material inside of the pants, but as he rubbed the material against itself, the stubborn pieces fell off along with the liquid matter that had erupted from him.

Satisfied with the level of filth remaining, Percy lifted the pants from the basin and began to strain the water from them. He knew it was a futile effort, but he had to get them as dry as possible. Murky water drained from between his clenched fists as he squeezed. The smell was starting to get to him. What had once been a turn-on was now utterly revolting. A gag caused his body to convulse. He slipped in the muck on the floor, nearly losing his balance.

As he continued to strain water from the sweats, he looked down at Rob. Soon, he would be in the news as "Officer Nelson" and Percy wondered what else they would say about him. Would they say he was found in the bathroom of a Chinese restaurant with his baton covered in another man's shit? No, not if he could help it.

He decided his pants wouldn't get any drier, and so he put them on. Next, he unlocked the stall and made his way to the paper towel dispenser. Not wanting to spread fingerprints all over the scene of the crime, he grabbed a paper towel for each hand and went back to the dead officer. Using the towels as mittens, he picked up the baton and stuck it up the dead man's ass until the handle was planted firmly in his crack. The sight of his own shit sliding down the black pole and gathering at Rob's ass triggered another spout of gagging and convulsion. Percy grabbed the dead weight of the corpse's hand and wrapped it around the base of the baton to show that he had done this to himself. Maybe the bit about the tank lid would raise questions, but there was nothing he could do about that now.

Percy was ready to get the hell out of there before he threw up all over the place, but first he had to get rid of one more piece of evidence. The spunk on the toilet seat would almost certainly be checked for DNA and had to be removed. With the brown wad of paper in his hand, he wiped it up and headed out of the stall with it. As he did so, his foot hit something that sent a metallic sound reverberating around the tiny stall: Nelson's police badge.

After a second of contemplation, Percy knelt and picked it up. In the stall beside Nelson, he washed off the badge before placing the come rag inside the bowl. The last step was to mop up the shit and filthy footprints he had left all over the bathroom and wipe the tank lid free of his fingerprints. If he could erase every sign of him ever having been there, it would increase his odds of getting off the hook for murdering a police officer. Nelson could remain in a puddle of shit and his own jism to be found by one of his buddies.

Drenched in sweat, Percy stood in front of the door, looking over the bathroom. With the stall door shut, nothing seemed amiss, aside from the puddle of blood and shit that was hardly visible. He gave his face a quick splash in the sink. Trying to look as casual as possible, he opened the door and put his hands into his pockets, feeling the badge as he did so. Closing his eyes momentarily, he took a deep breath before stepping out of the restroom.

The badge, which was now clenched in his fist, gave him a newfound sense of confidence as he exited. With his system freshly cleansed, he was lighter on his feet and sped through the dining area with urgency.

Walking into Percy's field of vision, the waiter, with hands full of dirty dishes, asked, "You want anything else?"

Percy pulled out the badge and replied, "Not now. I'm on official business. Thank you." He walked past the unmanned cash register at the front of the restaurant and out through the front doors.

He couldn't believe his luck. Had the waiter not recognized him?

Impossible! *I was the only customer in there . . .*

Percy made his way down the alley next to the restaurant and found a window. With great effort, he climbed onto a bin and pressed his face to the cold glass. He was wrong. There was a drunken party he had not noticed in the corner, along with a loved-up couple across from them. However, there was only the one waiter, and the chef, who was working in a kitchen visible to the customers, appeared busy.

It's possible only the waiter saw us.

Percy could almost hear the cogs in his mind clack as they turned with an idea.

A smile materialized on his face.

He jumped off the bin, causing shockwaves of pain to shoot through his knees, and then hobbled towards the restaurant's main door. Before going back inside, he made sure the street was quiet.

Again, Percy was in luck, as the waiter made his way towards him with a perplexed look on his face.

"Could you step this way, please," Percy said, putting his arm around the man and leading him towards the exit. The other diners and the cook were too engrossed in what they were doing to notice.

"What is this?!" the waiter asked.

"I just need you to come down to the station with me." Percy flashed Robert's badge again.

"I working. I can't go." He tried to stop walking, but Percy bundled him out the door by putting all his weight against the much smaller man.

"This won't take long, sir. Promise."

With that, Percy shoved the man outside and then down the alley and into a couple of bins. The waiter toppled over them with a cry, much to Percy's amusement.

"Oh, I'm sorry."

"Police brutality!" He was dragging himself along the ground when Percy stamped on his back. "*Argh!*"

"Stop resisting." Percy dragged the man to his feet and threw him against the wall opposite. With nobody around, he felt he could do whatever he pleased.

The waiter held his hands out in front of him. "I didn't do anything!"

In the spilled trash, Percy spotted a broken bottle. He went to it and swept it up with his fat hand. His stubby fingers closed around the intact neck.

"Why you doing this?"

"Shut up!" Percy turned on the man and shoved the jagged end of the bottle into his throat and twisted it. Strips of flesh came away when he retracted it. Blood squirted freely up the man's face, wall, and onto Percy, who stepped back quickly, fearing he would become drenched.

"Ugh-*uch!*" the man gargled.

As Percy watched the Asian man slip down the wall, he noticed the nametag he was wearing. "Chon," he read. "Huh. Fancy that?" He giggled. "I guess you're here one minute, and then *Chon* the next!"

When Chon's ass connected with the floor, he held out a bloody hand towards Percy. "H—h—help..." He gargled once, spat a gob of blood, and then died, sliding off to one side.

After covering the body with a pile of trash and placing a few bins around it, Percy fled the scene, using all the backstreets and roads he could where possible. Within two hours, he was back home and happy to find that his mother had gone for one of her afternoon naps after working a nightshift down at the morgue.

As quick as he could, Percy stripped out of his clothes, balled them up, and carried them into the bathroom with him. He then took a hot shower and made sure to clean the tub vigorously once he was finished, removing all traces of shit, blood, and anything else that had been clinging to him.

He bagged the clothes and threw them in the trash bin and put it outside, ready for tomorrow's collection.

When he was finished, Percy dressed in his PJs, made himself a cup of tea, and flopped in front of the television. He wasn't hungry; he'd had little appetite since walking into the Chinese restaurant earlier. The TV played on and on in the background and, even though he was looking at it, the moving images and sounds were lost on him.

Maybe I'm coming down with something? he wondered, sweat breaking across his brow.

No, he knew exactly what it was.

Guilt.

He'd been feeling it since he got out of the shower—his mind had become an unraveling mummy as he'd scrubbed the grime away, and fear had set in.

They're going to come for me and take me away.

They'll find my prints everywhere.

Someone will have seen me.

At one point, his heart started beating so fast that Percy feared it would explode in his chest, but he managed to calm himself and also stopped his bladder from emptying like a two-year-old's.

When his mother came into the room to inform him that she was leaving for work, it didn't register under the weight of his world collapsing around him.

"What have I done? What am I going to do?!"

"Excuse me?" his mother asked, rushing around the place. "Have you seen my purse, Percy?"

"Nothing, Mum . . ."

She said something else, but he didn't hear her. The next thing he knew, the front door slammed shut, breaking his trance.

"I could run!" He jumped out of his chair at the idea, knocking his mug of cold tea over. "But to where, and with what money?"

Mother has money, a voice at the back of his mind said.

His eyes glazed over, and his head tilted to one side. "Hmm . . . I've killed twice. Would a third make a difference?"

Percy couldn't believe what he was thinking. He was growing out of a perverted phase and into a lunatic. This wasn't him. However, his hand had been forced into doing awful things. And he knew he would have to do more horrible things to get out of his current situation.

His mind raced.

I could poison her?

Push her down the stairs?

Cut her throat?

Bash her brains in?

Even if he did kill her and take all her money, which she had stashed in the house because she didn't trust banks, there was nowhere to go. Also, what would he do with the body? Someone would find it after he'd fled and know he'd done it.

"Unless I tell people her and I are moving?" His heartbeat quickened. "I could disappear anywhere—the world, and everything in it, would be mine."

As excited as he was, Percy knew he couldn't do this half-cocked. He needed a plan, and a solid one at that.

First, he needed to sit tight and see if anything came of the murders he had already committed. If he murdered his mother and fled immediately, then they would put two and two together and realize he was behind it all.

They'd throw the book at him.

Percy needed to bide his time.

"I need to think of an escape . . ."

A jazzy, upbeat advertisement with flicky-flashy neon lights caught his attention like a slap to the face. When he looked at the screen, he saw half-naked women beckoning him with their fingers and come-to-bed eyes.

"Got the staying power for the adult entertainment industry?" the voiceover asked in a cheesy, seventies porn kind of way. It made Percy want to go to the front door to see if there was a plumber standing there with a drop handlebar moustache. "If you think you've got what it takes, with any kind of kink that you have, then call our production team on the number at the bottom of your screen. Casting begins next month, so don't delay. Call Carl's Casting Couch . . ."

"Trashy ad," he mumbled, throwing the TV remote to one side. "'With any kind of kink that you have,'" he mocked. "As If *I* could be a porno actor."

His stomach knotted, and a squeaky fart left his puckered anus. A small wave of pleasure washed over him as his guts flip-flopped and the pressure pushed against his internal g-spot.

"*Ugh!*" Percy fell into his chair and grabbed the arms with force. Since he hadn't eaten much of anything all day, he couldn't understand how another shit had built up. *Maybe it didn't all come out earlier?* he guessed.

His dick stiffened, and it wasn't long before come leaked out of its tip.

When he'd been in the bathroom standing over Robert's body and gagging at the smell, Percy had thought his perversion had gone away; that the stench, murder, and mayhem had placed a tint on his secret sexual desire.

He tried to get up, but a sudden explosion of pain in his guts rooted him to the spot.

"Oh, *fuck*!"

There was nothing he could do other than shit his pants this time.

As he forced the crap out, he came twice, soaking the front of his bottoms, which glued to his underwear, private parts, and pubes.

The excrement wasn't hard—it pissed out of him as though he was shitting through the eye of a needle and pooled around his feet.

When the episode was over and Percy was able to stand, he saw that his diarrhea had soaked through the chair and formed a neat puddle under the seat.

He laughed, then cleaned it up off the floor and scrubbed the seat clean.

As he showered for a second time, Percy thought more about the sleazy ad he'd seen on the TV and knew that his ass perversion gave credence to becoming an adult entertainment actor.

"They do all sorts of crazy, weird stuff in porn," he told himself, "including people crapping on each other, golden showers, snuff . . ."

The excitement returned by the time he got out of the shower and dressed in fresh pajamas.

"Carl's Casting Couch . . ." he said, returning to the living room and writing the name down on a piece of paper. "I should be able to find their number online."

When he realized it was past midnight, Percy decided to leave the searching until tomorrow.

I'll get on it first thing in the morning.

The following morning, Percy was awakened by his mother slamming the front door closed.

"Are you getting out of bed this morning, Percy?!" she cried in a venomous tone.

"Ugh!" He rolled over in bed and placed his pillow over his head. "The sooner she's fucking toes up, the better."

"Lazy bastard," Percy heard her say, which was followed by another door thumping shut.

Bitch got a mood on her today. Maybe one of the stiffs tried it on with her. The thought brought a smile to his face. *Those poor fuckers on the slab are already cold enough, without trying to get it on with a frigid fuck like her.*

He doubted a trip through the ovens at her workplace would heat her up.

And then it hit him:

Burn her remains!

She had keys to the place. He could follow her there one night soon, kill her, and then dispose of her body and grind her bones to dust.

That's ingenious. He bounced out of bed and paced. *That could really work. I just need to get my plan organized and research cremation.*

I also need to make sure I can get in with Carl. If not Carl, then another porn agency.

When he finally managed to calm himself, Percy sat at his PC and researched Carl's and the cremation process. In between this, he kept his eye on the news and scanned the internet to see if the police had any new information.

So far, they had nothing. No eyewitness, prints, or an idea of who could have carried out the heinous murders.

When nobody came knocking at Percy's door over the course of the following few weeks, it led him to believe that he was in the clear. The authorities were never coming, leaving him to carry out his plan with his mother and escape his humdrum life.

Six months later, with a plan fully formed, Percy was ready to strike.

Over the time it had taken him to construct his scheme, many things had happened. For starters, the police had arrested someone for the murders he'd committed: a homeless man by the name of Benedict Johnston, who had walked into the police station and spilled his guts.

At first, the arresting officer had been skeptical, even though Johnston had known things about the murders that only the authorities knew, details which had not been relayed to the media. However, when pressed for further information, the supposed killer started coming unstuck, leading the officer to think that the man was trying to get himself taken in so he'd have a permanent bed and three hot meals a day.

When it looked as though they were going to escort Benedict off the premises, he'd drawn the officer's gun and fired four shots into the cop's chest, killing him outright.

The whole situation had brought a glorious smile to Percy's face.

Another significant thing which had happened was that Percy had landed three separate interviews for companies within the adult entertainment industry. After telling them all about his unusual turn-on, they'd been very interested in seeing him, which pleased him to no end—when he'd tried Carl's, they'd turned him down immediately.

He'd walked into the first interview a bag of nerves. Getting the job and not being able to put his plans into action hadn't worried him, but discussing his perverted fantasy with an interviewer had.

When he'd walked out of the box-sized room forty minutes later, he'd been happy with how it had gone, which gave him hope that he could land the job and move on with his life. But after he received a call with bad news, Percy was about ready to go back on the life he had dreamed up for himself.

"What's it matter? Cops ain't looking for me."

Still, he went to the second interview, and failed that one, too.

Unlike the first time, he didn't let this deter him. With a month in between the botched second attempt and the final interview, Percy prepared by making sure he had a huge load of shit built up inside him. The first interview had failed because he hadn't had waste to eject when they'd asked to see what he could do. The second had gone south because he hadn't been able to perform when they'd asked.

If the third time isn't my charm, it will surely be my doom!

He took some deep breaths through his nose and let them out through his mouth. These were his last-ditch efforts at turning his life around and truly starting anew. After the first two interviews—and subsequent rejections—his confidence had somehow begun to bud rather than whither. He felt as though he had a better sense of what the producers wanted and believed he would be able to give it to them. He thought he would be able to perform in front of others this time.

His mother, on the other hand, was a different story. Over the weeks, he'd been trying to get in her good graces—something far more difficult than he had initially surmised. Not only did she continue to treat him as though he was acting the same way he always had, but she also seemed quite skeptical at every nice thing he did. Being nice was the most painful chore he had ever had the displeasure of doing, and the fact that he couldn't get the old bitch to smile was a swift kick to the sack.

A vibration from his hip pocket jarred him from his train of thought. He reached his hand in and withdrew his phone. The word *CUNT* ran across the top of the screen. He sighed. He hated playing nice. He even had to change the inflection of his voice to avoid conveying his annoyance. "Hiya, Ma."

"Percy, my boy, I forgot to bring my lunch. I was hoping you could bring it by in a few hours."

Percy clenched his teeth together. As much as he did not want to go anywhere today, he absolutely had to say yes so he could gain access to the mortuary and deal her in. This was it: his golden ticket to the end of the awful twat! "Oh, yes! Of course, Mother. Wouldn't want you to get famished while out making a living for the two of us. The brown bag in the refrigerator, I presume?"

"Really? You'll do that for me? Oh, Percy, you *are* a good boy! I didn't think it was possible this late in the game, but you really are changing for the better, aren't you?!"

For once, he felt a bitter joy resulting from being nice to the bitch. "I can't answer that for you, Mother—only time can." Thoughts of her body roasting over an open flame filled his mind. The image of fire coupled with his overwhelming excitement caused him to break out in a sweat.

"Well, I gotta get back to it," she said, a smile coming through in her voice. "Thank you so much, my baby boy! I'll see you in just a couple hours. Kisses!"

His stomach flip-flopped as he repeated the word before ending the call.

Fantastic! I can bring her—

His thoughts were interrupted by another phone call coming through, this time from *UNKNOWN CALLER*.

The fuck is this? he thought, putting the phone back up to his face. "Who is this?"

"Percival James?" a rough voice said. There was no sound in the background.

"Who's asking?" Percy's anus tightened at the possibility of the police having found him out.

"I understand you're looking to get into the online kink scene, is that so?"

A sense of relief washed over him. "Yeah, that's right." Like a hungry wolf, he licked his lips in anticipation. "Do you have something for me?"

"Perhaps. Can you come for an interview right now?" The voice had no trace of emotion, as if it had been programmed by a computer.

A smile burst across his mouth at the words, somber though they were. "Yeah, I absolutely can!" He looked at the time on his phone and saw that it was already ten o'clock. "Actually, is there any chance of doing this later in the day? Or perhaps tomorrow morning?"

"No. It's now or not at all."

Percy could hear the dull-voiced man take a drag from a cigarette or cigar. His shoulders drooped. Either the murder or his future career would have to be potentially put on hold. *Or maybe I can go to the interview and finish up in time to go to the mortuary and do her in*! "No, you're right. Now or never. I can head your direction at once. Where is it you're located?"

"Are you familiar with the convenience store across from the bus station down on Main?"

"Yes, I believe so."

"If you walk around back, you'll find an alleyway that leads to us. We're behind two dumpsters and a black Mercedes. Be here in fifteen minutes."

Percy pulled the phone from his head and saw that the call had been ended.

He sat up on his bed, found his sweatpants that were nearby, and slid into them. His heart was filled with what he assumed was joy. *I can go to the audition and blow them away with the beast I've been brewing. Once they see Ol' Faithful, there's no chance they won't want to see it again!* With such an unusual kink, he thought he might become the star of the fetish. And after he nailed the audition, he'd take a quick bus trip to the mortuary and dispose of the old witch. Oh, this was going to be one of the best days of his life!

Percy left the building with a speed he had not reached since his high school days. If he wasn't concerned about breaking his legs in the process, he would've been in a flat-out sprint to the street. As luck had it, there was a taxi cab just outside, dropping off a fair. "Taxi!" he shouted, flailing his arms in the air. *"Taxi!"*

The cab driver saw Percy through the window and waved in acknowledgement. He slowed his pace some, but not much. When he finally reached the vehicle, he popped his head into the open window and said, "Main Street, and step on it!" before getting settled in the back seat.

"Thanks a lot, buddy," Percy said, passing the man a twenty-dollar bill through the window.

"I said twenty-five thirty-eight!" the cab driver shouted angrily at Percy's back.

To this, he simply replied with a smile that the driver would not see, and an extended middle finger that he wouldn't be able to miss.

There were no cars in the convenience store parking lot Percy was walking toward, but a few crackheads and other homeless people lurked. "Ach, and I thought that last shit I took stunk," he said, trying to get a rise out of the human trash staring him down. Without incident, though, he walked through the empty lot and alongside the building. Somehow, it smelled even worse here, and the stench seemed to worsen the farther back he went.

About halfway to the end of the building, his nerves kicked in. He felt queasy and began to doubt the actual likelihood of him being able to perform as he had hoped. A fart of dreadful woe made a slow escape from his sweatpants. The hot stench that followed put the smell of the filthy homeless people to shame. "There, there, stomach. Being nervous is what got us in trouble the last two times. Let's go see the nice people and just try to have a good time. That's really all they want to see, isn't it? The 'normal' people out there like to wank off while watching others enjoy themselves. Why on God's green Earth that's more fun to watch than people in agony is beyond me, but we just want to give the people what they want." He patted his stomach. His gut replied with a grumble of contentedness.

Now feeling like part of a team, Percy walked with a sense of swagger along the back of the building toward the black Mercedes that was parked near some trash cans. He put his hands in his pockets and whistled an upbeat tune as he went.

Two men were inside the car. With a big smile and a wave, Percy greeted them. "Hiya, fellas!" he said to the rolled-up window.

The man in the driver's seat looked over at him before nudging his partner. Once the second man had a chance to look him over, the two spoke for a moment— Percy thought it sounded Russian, though it was muffled through the glass. Eventually, the one in the driver's seat nodded and they exited the vehicle.

Without saying a word, the driver lit up a cigarette and motioned toward the alley beside the trash cans.

"Of course," said Percy, moving to his spot. "I gotta tell ya, I feel a bit like a sixteen-year-old girl who just got her first taste of cock and thinks it's her ticket to a million dollars." A chortle escaped him. "Of course, my tits could look nicer and my hair could have a little more volume and I don't think I'll ever be a millionaire, but you get the drift."

"Ты человек, который срёт?" (You're the man who shits?), the man from the passenger seat asked.

Percy looked from one man to the next. "I'm ready to get started whenever you guys are." He was now growing very uneasy and beginning to wonder what the hell he was doing coming to a place like this as vulnerable as a schoolgirl still in pigtails.

The driver struck the passenger on the shoulder and shook his head. Then he looked to Percy, placed the cigarette between his lips, and gestured to his ass with both hands.

Percy made the same gesture. "Shit? From my ass? You want me to shit?" he asked, nodding along. He moved his right hand to his cock, leaving the left hand in back. "Shit and jerk off? You want me to get started right now?"

The two men smiled and nodded. "Да. Дерьмо." (Yes. Shit.)

"Ok!" Percy said, clapping his hands together. A genuine smile returned to his face. He felt as though things might turn out okay after all.

He watched as the passenger opened the back door of the car and pulled out a tripod.

"Wait, wait, wait," Percy said, waving his hands in front of him. "I thought this was just an interview. Are we going to be filming this too?" He pointed to the tripod, then held his hands up in front of his face to indicate a camera.

"Movie. Yes," said the driver, nodding.

"If we're already making a movie, I'm going to need to get paid. I might enjoy what I do, but I want to get paid for it. That's the whole point of my being here today."

The look on the man's face made it obvious he didn't understand a single word.

Percy rubbed his thumb in a circular motion against his index and middle fingers. "Money." He pointed down at the ground. "Now."

The driver nodded. Then, he opened the passenger side door, sat down, and opened the glovebox. Percy saw several stacks of banded bills before the man grabbed the nearest one and slammed the small door shut once more.

Percy enjoyed watching the momentary struggle the driver had with gravity as he rocked himself out of the seat. Once he finally stood, he tossed the cash down at Percy's feet. "Movie."

After kneeling and picking up the unknown amount of money, Percy nodded and repeated the word: "Movie."

The cameraman pointed toward a flat piece of cardboard near the dumpster and shouted, "Now!"

Percy, still nodding, put the bundle of cash into his sweatpants pocket and strode toward the already filthy cardboard. The smile faded from his face as his olfactory sense was overwhelmed. The stench that he had thought was coming from the dirty hobos was actually coming from these dumpsters. He held back a gag that nearly made some of the shit spill from his anus, were it not for his quick sphincter reflexes.

Still, he didn't want to fuck this up. This was likely the end of the road for the life he wanted. If he were to screw up this final interview, he may never get another chance. Shitting and jerking off on camera—even the thought of it made his dick hard, despite the horrendous surroundings. If there were more wads of money like this in the business, he'd better make goddamn sure he gave it his all!

"So, do I just . . ." He trailed off once he got on top of the flat cardboard. He wasn't sure what the stains were, but they appeared to be on the cardboard and the blacktop. *I'm not the first one to shit on here and I probably won't be the last. It's just part of the gig, Perc!*

"Movie!" shouted the cameraman, pointing a frustrated finger at Percy.

"Right," he said, trying to get himself in the right frame of mind. "Time to make sexy." He grabbed the bottom of his shirt and slowly pulled it over his head, wiggling his hips back and forth to make himself look more appealing.

The driver nudged the cameraman. Percy couldn't hear what he said, and it likely wouldn't have mattered if he had, but it looked like he was pleased with the way this was going.

Next, Percy turned around and reached down to untie his shoes, his hairy tits sagging as he did so. He looked between his legs, reaching his left hand through to poke at his asshole while looking playfully at the camera. The smiles on the face of the men watching him caused his erection to stiffen even more.

"You like that, fellas?" he asked. "You filthy fucks!"

His hand slowly retracted from his hole and moved to the front of the waistband along with his other hand. Together, they slid down the top of the sweats. He alternated sides, dropping the material gathered on each hip incrementally. He felt giddy as his ass crack emerged from its hiding place.

His stomach felt more aroused than his cock. The shit that had built up inside was tremendous. The length of time he had spent brewing this one and the meticulous nature with which he'd formed it were sure to pay off when it was finally time to unload.

He turned around to face the camera and kicked off each boot—they each flew right past the ears of the man filming. His erection was being tugged down along with the waistband. With a gentle pull forward of the elastic, the hard-on was set free, springing forth like a jack in the box. Percy wore the face of an innocent young boy not knowing what he was doing.

The driver opened the rear door of the car and sat down, clearly looking for something. Percy didn't want it to distract him, so he spun around once more. This time, he pulled the sweats all the way down, revealing that he had somehow tucked his genitals between his legs to expose them to the camera.

"There we have it, kids," he said, careening his neck around. Behind the cameraman, he saw the other Russian still digging in the back seat for something.

What if he's looking for a fucking gun? Percy thought in a fleeting moment. Then, he told himself there was nothing to worry about. These guys were loving everything he did and they hadn't even seen the main attraction yet. Besides, this wasn't a snuff film or anything like that. It was a legit porno company.

He stood, caressing himself between his legs, back still turned to the camera. A pain struck him in the guts. "Okay, guys. It's just about time for Old Faithful to blow. If I was a watermelon-smashing comedian, now would be the time I'd advise you to pull up your plastic sheets."

Percy spread his feet out to a wider stance as he continued to stroke himself. The bubbling feeling inside caused his cock to pulsate with pleasure. Suddenly, all the filth and ugliness he had been holding in from the world ejected itself from his body. It coated his feet and ankles, and splashed up on his calves and even his inner thighs.

His asshole wasn't the only thing to unleash all it had held back. His front let open its floodgates as well. Pearly white drops of come fired down in spurts into the growing puddle of shit like scud missiles, sending minor shockwaves radiating outward from the point of impact.

The act took everything out of Percy, who collapsed to his knees in the disgusting pool of bodily waste. His left hand extended to the ground for support, while his right hand continued to rub his genitals and asshole. Not only was this quite possibly the best shit *and* the best orgasm of his life, but he had done it all on camera. He had done it in front of the people that would make him rich. He had done one of the two prerequisites that would allow him to pass on to his next stage of life. All that stood in his way now was his mother.

Down in the muck, his look of pure satisfaction was replaced by a devious smile once more. With the stack of cash and a promising career ahead of him, it was time to bring his mother her final meal.

The sound of hurried footsteps snapped him back to the here and now. He looked over to the cameraman, who had turned the camera away from him and onto the driver, who was now armed with a machete.

"Wha-What is this?" Percy shoved himself off the ground and stood. Liquid feces trailed down his legs and arms—his right hand was covered in semen. He backed up rapidly, trying to get away from the chipped and shabby-looking blade. "Hey, man, listen: I don't know what type of film you think this is going to be or exactly who it is you think you're *fucking* with," he said, voice growing louder and more aggressive, "but that knife needs to disappear before it finds its way into your asshole!"

Percy's bare ass cheeks bounced into the wall of the building behind him. The brick was cold and rough on his shit-covered skin. His heart raced even faster than before. "I don't want any trouble here, you hear me? I just want to take my money and leave so that I can shower and bring my mother her lunch. If you keep this up, you won't be the first stupid piece of shit I've killed in my time, do you understand?"

If he did understand it, he did a fantastic job of hiding it.

Percy looked to the cameraman, who was following their every move. "Fucking call this guy off or he's going to get it!" He moved sideways along the wall, trying like hell to find anything that would keep him out of harm's way.

There was nothing in that direction but a dead-end.

"Help! Help me!" he shouted at the top of his lungs.

The only answers came in the form of distorted echoes bouncing off the walls around him.

Seeing that no one was going to interfere with this matter, Percy decided to make a run for it. He darted off down the dark alley, careful not to slip in the fecal matter caked to the bottom of his feet.

The two men gave chase. The camera shot out a beam of light, which caught Percy off guard. He turned his head to gauge how fast the other men were. It didn't matter: his feet skidded on the shit-soaked cardboard that was in his path, throwing him off balance. His great mass fell to the ground, shattering his coccyx upon impact.

"Fuck, fuck, fuck, fuck!" The searing pain shot straight up his spine but was nothing compared to the knowledge that he was about to be brutally murdered.

As the blade drew nearer and nearer to his throat, the pain that filled his body and the fear that filled his mind were somehow the most erotic things he had ever experienced.

A stream of jizz spewed forth as the blade sliced into his throat.

Other HellBound Books Titles

Available at: www.hellboundbookspublishing.com

Man Eating F*cks
By
David Owain Hughes

A dark, incredibly entertaining excursion into the delightfully twisted imagination of David Owain Hughes....

An average teenage girl and her father find themselves caught up in a brutal nightmare at their local recreational centre, when an age-old enemy comes stumbling out of the woods to crash a heavy-metal gig; a gig that has all the promises of being killer. This is one blood-soaked gig you won't want to miss!

Praise for Man-Eating F*cks from Ty Schwamberger (author of The Fields, Deep Dark Woods & The Death of a Horror Writer.) "Man Eating F*cks is old school horror, but with a new, blood-soaked twist! David Owain Hughes effectively creates enjoyable and lethal characters in this tale that is sure to keep you up at night. This is the type of tale that you need to read with a light on…I'm serious. You better put your seatbelt on 'cause you're in for one helluva ride. Look out, Hughes might very well be headed to the major leagues after this twisted tale! Highly recommended!"

Psychological Breakdown
By
David Owain Hughes

COMING OCTOBER 2017 from HellBound Books!

Within this tome lies eighteen tales of mind-bending terror, as Hughes delves into the human psyche and dishes out stories of what becomes of the broken minded, spirited and downright irked.

Part these blood-drenched pages at your own peril, for you will find diseased minds geared towards revenge and bloody chaos, with a few twists, turns and surprises thrown in for good, fucked-up measures.

Keep the lights on!

Worship Me

Something is listening to the prayers of St. Paul's United Church, but it's not the god they asked for; it's something much, much older.

A quiet Sunday service turns into a living hell when this ancient entity descends upon the house of worship and claims the congregation for its own. The terrified churchgoers must now prove their loyalty to their new god by giving it one of their children or in two days time it will return and destroy them all.

As fear rips the congregation apart, it becomes clear that if they're to survive this untold horror, the faithful must become the faithless and enter into a battle against God itself. But as time runs out, they discover that true monsters come not from heaven or hell...

...they come from within.

No Rest For The Wicked

A modern day ghost story with its skeletons buried firmly in the past.

From beyond the grave, a murderous wife seeks to complete her revenge on those who betrayed her in life; a powerless domestic still fears for her immortal soul while trying to scare off anyone who comes too close; and the former plantation master - a sadistic doctor who puts more faith in the teachings of de Sade than the Bible

When Eric and Grace McLaughlin purchase Greenbrier Plantation, their dreams are just as big as those who have tried to tame the place before them. But, the doctor has learned a thing or two over his many years in the afterlife, is putting those new skills to the test, and will go to great lengths in order to gain the upper hand. While Grace digs into the death-filled history of her new home, Eric soon becomes a pawn of the doctor's unsavory desires and rapidly growing power, and is hell-bent on stopping her.

The Amnesia Girl

Filled with copious amounts of black humor, Gerri R. Gray's first published novel is an offbeat adventure story that could be described as One Flew over the Cuckoo's Nest meets Thelma and Louise.

Flashback to 1974. Farika is a lovely young woman who wakes up one day to find herself a patient in a bizarre New York City psychiatric asylum. She has no idea who she is, and possesses no memories of where she came from nor how she got there.

Fearing for her life after being attacked by a berserk girl with over one hundred personalities and a vicious nurse with sadistic intentions, the frightened amnesiac teams up with an audacious lesbian with a comically unbalanced mind, and together they attempt a daring escape.

But little do they know that a long strange journey into an even more insane world filled with a multitude of perilous predicaments and off-kilter individuals are waiting for them on the outside. Farika's weird reality crumbles when she finally discovers who, and what, she really is!

The Cabin Sessions

The Cabin Sessions is a confronting, hard-hitting dark psychological thriller, told with an acid wit. Themes of domestic and child abuse are explored through minds distorted by fear, and corrupted by hatred and delusion. A tale where redemption is gained in unexpected ways.

It's Christmas Eve when hapless musician Adam Banks stands on the bridge over the river that cleaves the isolated village of Burton. A storm is rolling into the narrow mountain pass. He thinks of turning back. Instead, he resolves to fulfill his obligation to perform the guest spot at The Cabin Sessions. He should be looking forward to it, but fear stirs when he opens the door on the Cabin's incense-choked   air.

Meanwhile, Philip's sister, Eva, prepares to take a bath. It's a ritual. She's a breath holder. At twenty-eight she's returned to Burton to finish the business of her past; business she must attend to, if only she could make sense of it. Memories begin to surface concerning the innocence of her brother.

Blood and Kisses

The definitive short story collecting from James H Longmore - an eclectic mix of dark horror, bizarro and Twilight-Zone style tales of the downright disturbing.

Welcome to the long awaited collection from the writer of horror novels *'Pede* and *Tenebrion*; a forword by Richard Chizmar (co-author of *Gwendy's Button Box* and author of *A Long December*), 18 short stories, 5 flash fiction and even a poem - all skin-crawling, soul-shredding tales of terror, of the darkest things that skulk amongst the night's inky shadows, and of the everyday gone horribly awry.

Discover the alternative implication of technology becoming self-aware, enjoy the acquaintance of a charismatic new pastor who promises his flock a brand new place in which to worship his God, and spend a little time in the company of a nice young man who is inexorably caught up in his home town's terrible secret. Then there is Cupid's revelation that personally he has never experienced love, yet we discover that very emotion alive and not so well amongst the ruins of a post zombie apocalypse world, and we bear witness to a childhood innocence forever destroyed in a war-torn city. There is more, Dear Reader, much, much more; for within these pages we have devils, demons and ghosts, lycanthropes and demi-gods, all rubbing nefarious shoulders with vilest of Hell's offspring who have slithered from the netherworld to doff their caps and wish us all the sweetest of dreams…

The Big Book of Bootleg Horror 2

The second volume in HellBound Books' flagship horror anthology - this one bursting at the seams with even more fantastically dark horror from the cream of the rising stars in today's horror scene!

Featuring: Tracey A. Cross, Elizabeth Zemlicka, Shelby Thomas, Matthew Gillies, Spinster Eskie, Stephen Clements, Ken Goldman, Nathan Robinson, K.M. Campbell, Cody Grady, Sebastian Bendix, Leo X. Robertson, David Owain Hughes, Timothy McGivney, Kane Gordon, Todd Sullivan, Mike Mayak, Edward Ahern, Rose Garnett, Jaap Boekestein, Brandy Delight, Stanley B. Webb, D. Norfolk, and Thomas Gunther.

David Owain Hughes & Peter Oliver Wonder

**A HellBound Books LLC
Publication**

http://www.hellboundbookspublishing.com

Printed in the United States of America